"YOU GOT THIS!"

GUIDE TO SUCCESSFULLY SURVIVING MIDDLE SCHOOL GUIDE

TYBREAI GARCIA

YOU GOT THIS!

GUIDE TO SUCCESSFULLY SURVIVING MIDDLE SCHOOL

Copyright © 2020 by TyBreai Garcia

To contact the author, email her mother Latasha Watkins at
tashawatkins2018@gmail.com

All rights reserved. No portion of this book may be reproduced, stored in a retrieval system, or transmitted in any form or by any means—electronic, mechanical, photocopy, recording, scanning, or other—except for brief quotations in critical reviews or articles, without the prior written permission of the publisher.

ZYIA CONSULTING
Illuminate & Transcend

Zyia Consulting
Book Writing & Publishing Company
www.nyishaddavis.com
nyisha.d.davis@gmail.com
678-881-5983

ISBN: 9798581484050

Printed in the United States of America.

Dedication

Dedicated to all the upcoming and current middle schoolers.

Acknowledgment

I thank my auntie, Edna Boyd Jones, for believing in me, discovering this opportunity, and making sacrifices so I could become a published author at the age of fourteen.

I would also like to thank my mother, Latasha Watkins, who gave me helpful suggestions and was there every day to encourage me to stay on track with my school work and writing.

I would like to acknowledge my grandmother Renee Cushman & great grandmother, Delores Mitchell, for their constant encouragement through words of wisdoms and perseverance.

I would also like to extend my gratitude to Ms. Davis, my writing coach, for giving me the opportunity to experience writing my own book. Without you, none of this would be possible.

Table of Content

Introduction

Chapter 1 - Friends

Chapter 2 - Bullying

Chapter 3 - Time Management

Chapter 4 - After School Activities

Chapter 5 - Independence

Chapter 6 - Self Image

Chapter 7 - The Bounce Back

Introduction

Middle school may get hard at times, but with this guide, you will receive a ton of helpful tips to get you through it. I wanted to write this book because many things changed that I was not ready for as I transitioned from elementary to middle school; friends, homework, peer pressure, and more. It is full of numerous challenging adventures, but it's also about finding the joy in it. With knowledge of the new things that you may encounter, you will be aware of them when or if these times come, and they will not affect you as badly.

This guide will teach you ways to survive middle school. The overall goal is to help middle school students be successful. As you read, I have listed things you can practice being successful. Practice them and check them off as you began to make them a part of your middle school life. You will also have a place to journal about your thoughts or experience with things in each chapter.

Chapter 1

Friends

Old and New Friends

When transitioning from elementary to middle school, you will meet many new people. Not all of your friends from elementary will be in middle school with you. Some may move away, while others may go to a different school. It's good to make new friends because you're going to need positive support. Having friends is a great way to receive that. As your middle school years go along, you may notice that your friends may find other friends or form other friend groups. This is normal, and if you guys are truly right for one another, you'll always find a way back with each other.

Peer Pressure

You may run into situations where you feel like you're being pressured to do something you know is not right or something you don't want to do. This is what is called "peer pressure." Now there are two types of peer pressure; positive and negative. Negative peer pressure is when one of your peers pressure you to do a certain action without you really being willing to do it.

Negative peer pressure example:

- An individual wanting to feel accepted in a friend group, so they do whatever they're told to do, such as smoking or doing another student's homework, just to be accepted.

Negative peer pressure will always pressure you to do things that will bring negative consequences. When/if you were to ever run into a situation similar to this, here are some tips to help you deal with it:

- Choose friends carefully
- Think ahead
- Get help from a trusted adult.
- Say no

Positive peer pressure is when someone is encouraging you to do something for a good cause.

Positive peer pressure example:

- An individual wants to accomplish a task and do not have the courage. They listen to positive advice and complete the task and have a healthy outcome.

To make sure you receive positive peer pressure, surround yourself with good friends who remind you to do what is right. When you receive positive peer pressure, you become more determined on what you want to do in the future.

Drama

When facing drama in middle school, it is really determined by the crowd you hang around. This is why you want to surround yourself with friends that have positive energy. You should never let someone else's drama affect you.

When dealing with drama:

- You can always walk away from it.
- Get help from adults if it gets serious.
- Stand up for yourself.

One of the most important things to remember is to keep important things to yourself. Only share these things with those who have gained your trust. If you tell certain peers about your situation, rumors can start, and it could make the situation worse. Keep in mind, it does take time to learn who you can trust. When dealing with drama and friends, they will most likely come and go, but the real friends will always stay.

Being honest is also key. For example, if you tell your friend that you can't go to a game because you have to study for a test, but you're actually going to another friend's sleepover, that could cause trouble.

A big role when dealing with drama is being the bigger person. You can always ignore and act like you don't care about what someone says about you. When the person sees that it does not bother you, they will most likely stop causing trouble with you because you're not feeding into the drama, and they are not receiving attention. You are unique, and everyone is different in their own way. So do not worry about the students who have negative opinions about you that make you feel bad.

Journal

Chapter 2

Bullying

Cyber

Examples of cyberbullying are sending hurtful messages and posting negative things about peers. When posting things on social media, even though you may delete it, it's always there forever. This is why you need to be very careful about posting certain things on the internet. Being a victim of cyberbullying, can be a stressful experience. It can lead to depression, low self-esteem, anxiety, and much more. When dealing with cyberbullying, there are many ways to cope with it.

A few things you can do if you find yourself in this situation:

- Block the bully
- Ignore the bully
- Make a report to the website.
- Tell a trusted adult.

Verbal

When people think of bullying, they may only think of cyber or physical (the most common ones), but verbal can be just as harmful. The definition of verbal bullying is when someone uses hurtful words towards their peers to make them feel down about themselves; teasing and insulting.

In a situation that involves verbal bullying, the main thing you can do is to:

- Walk away. This can stop things from escalating.
- Be confident. This lets the bully know that you aren't scared of them, and then hopefully, they will stop.

If the bullying continues, you can always go to a trusted adult such as your parent, teacher, and/or guidance counselor.

Physical

Physical bullying is one of the biggest problems that middle schoolers deal with today. Just as well as the other forms of bullying. It can lead to many negative outcomes, such as bodily harm, depression, suicide, anxiety, low self-esteem, and fear. This form of bullying involves hitting, tripping, pushing, stealing one's possessions, etc.

If these types of actions are continuously being repeated, you can try to:

- Avoid the bully as much as possible.
- Walk away and go to a safe place where teachers are present.
- Tell someone you trust
- Stand up for yourself.

Journal

Chapter 3

Time Management

Planning

In middle school, you will realize that you'll have a lot more homework than in elementary. You will be on your own to complete and turn in assignments, study for tests, and complete projects. You are going to be more independent.

Here are a few things that you can do to be successful:

- Have an agenda
- Do not do assignments at the last minute.

Using your time wisely should be number one on your agenda. If you get behind with your work, it will make things stressful. Planning is a great way to manage your time. Also, write down your assignments and use everything your teachers give and tell you to your advantage. It will keep you organized and on track. This way, you will not forget to study for a test, turn in an assignment, and prepare for future due dates.

Schedules

There's a huge difference with schedules in middle school. You will have up to seven classes in different classrooms. You will only have a few minutes to get from one classroom to another. You will have a locker instead of a desk to keep all of your books in. I suggest that you get the books you need for the first half of the day from your locker in the morning before school starts. After lunch, you should get the books you need for the rest of the day. This can help reduce tardiness.

You will most likely have a binder for each subject. You could color-code your binders. For example, for Science, you might want to use a blue binder. This is so you don't have to waste time trying to figure out which binder is for which class.

Discipline

Since middle school gives you more freedom and independence, discipline needs to be taken seriously. You want to set a good reputation for yourself, because in the long run it's going to benefit you. If teachers see that you cause trouble and aren't really taking your work seriously, they will not give you second chances if you need extra work to make your grade higher. When you set a bad reputation for yourself, you miss out on great opportunities. You never know who's watching, so you always want to do your best at all times.

Stress

Stress is a major problem. You can be greatly affected by stress due to the many changes you encounter in middle school. Some common stressors could be your new homework loads, grades, peer pressure, and more.

Some ways to help deal with stress:

- Stay organized
- Do not take on too many projects or join too many groups or clubs at one time.
- Time management is also a big key to reducing stress.

Other ways to keep your stress level low is to:

- Get enough sleep

- Eat healthy
- Exercise
- Do positive things you love to do; singing, dancing, playing games, spending time with family, etc.

Journal

Chapter 4

After School Activities

As you're learning to become more independent in middle school, it's important that you make decisions that benefit you best. Being involved in after school activities, helps you to succeed in your independence. These activities can help you find what interests you most while also keeping you active within your school.

Studies say that after school activities also help improve grades, as well as your confidence. Although there are many benefits of after-school activities, there can also be some negative outcomes if you don't manage your time wisely.

Always remember that no matter what after school activities you participate in, make time for your studies. Many teams make you keep a certain average to be a part of it, so it's very important that you keep up with your studies as well.

Journal

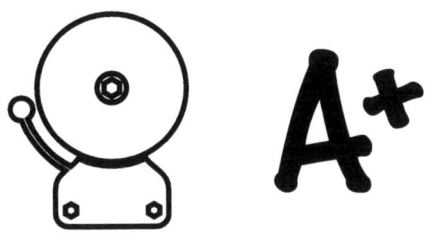

Chapter 5

Independence

The Bell

Middle school requires you to be more independent and very organized. Most middle schools have something known as "the bell." It sounds when it's time for school to start and when it's time to go from one class to another. There are usually two bells before each class. One is a signal to start class, and the second one tells you that you should already be seated in class.

Unlike elementary school, where you stayed in one class and walked with your teacher everywhere, you walk to your class alone with little supervision in middle school. This is where independence comes along. You're being trusted enough to walk to class and get there on time. This is preparing you for the future; college and a career.

Grades

Work does tend to become harder, but it's still very important to keep your grades up. You wouldn't want to fall into the habit of getting bad grades because it follows you into high school. One way of maintaining good grades is staying organized. If you're not organized, this could lead to losing assignments, forgetting to do homework, being unprepared for tests, missing practice, and more.

Another way of maintaining good grades is by using your time wisely. It can be very easy to become distracted when doing assignments, projects, and homework. If you don't use your time wisely, you can start falling behind on things that are due. This can lead to unnecessary stress.

Behavior

Your behavior in middle school is critical. One, it can set your reputation for following you into high school. Since you are older now and hold a bigger responsibility for your actions, negative behavior can lead to serious consequences such as detention, suspension, and more. You always want to try to be the best you that you can be, because your behavior affects you in the long run. For example, if you do really badly on a test and want to see if you can do extra credit work to bring up your grade, if you have behavior problems, the teacher may feel like you don't deserve a second chance. You always want to stay on the teacher's good side.

Study Groups

Study groups can be very helpful. You can quiz one another before the test. Another benefit is the communication within your study group. It will keep you organized and remind you about test days. Being a part of a study group, you have to stay focused and be very committed. It can be easy to get off track, especially if you and your friends are a part of the same group. You have to try your hardest to make it strictly about studying and nothing else. If you get off track, you will waste time, and then you won't gain what you need to help you prepare for upcoming assignments and tests.

Journal

Chapter 6
Self Image

You Are Unique

EVERYONE is different. No one is the same. We all have something unique about ourselves that no one else has. Nowadays, many people try to change themselves to fit into a certain group and look the same. Always remember, just be yourself! If you feel that you have to fit in with the crowd, you'll always change yourself to accomplish that because you'll never accept you for you. Being different from other people is really an advantage. One advantage of being unique is being able to stand out from other people. You don't want to be the same as everybody else. You want to be your own person with your own personality and creativity. If you like doing certain things, then do them. Make sure it is something positive that will give you positive outcomes. Don't try to please other people because 90% of the time, you won't see them again when you graduate from middle school or high school. Do what makes you happy. Be proud about it!

Self Esteem - High and Low

What is self-esteem? Self-esteem is the way a person views themself. There are two types of self-esteem; low and high. Many teens today face low-self esteem. This can lead to horrible outcomes such as depression, suicide, low grades, and more. When having high-self esteem, you're confident in yourself.

Ways you can build yourself up:

- Make a list of things you love about yourself.
- Ask your family and trusted friends to tell you good things about you.
- Surround yourself with positive people
- Set goals and working towards them

It can be effortless to look at all the negative things, but if you focus more on the positive, you can have more confidence, higher self-esteem, and find yourself to be happier.

Self Love

If you don't remember anything else, always remember that self-love is the best love! It's key to your mental health. It helps reduce depression, anxiety, and much more. If you make mistakes, it's okay to forgive yourself. I feel as though if you never love yourself, you can never be at peace with yourself. By this, I mean you may never know what you need mentally and physically to become a better you.

Journal

Chapter 7

The Bounce Back

Now that you've been given advice on how to survive middle school successfully, you can apply this knowledge, be well prepared, and succeed. I know for a fact that if you be yourself, use your time wisely, and have courage; you'll be more than successful! Middle school is all about preparing you to find who you are and what you want to do in the future. In elementary, they always held your hand, but not in middle school.

Yes, there are going to be times where it gets challenging and you make mistakes. But remember that there are brighter days ahead, and learn from your mistakes and their consequences. Everyone makes mistakes and it's not the end of the world. Always remember to have fun because overwhelming yourself with more than what you can handle can lead to stress and much more! Middle school is mainly a way of teaching you to become more organized and makes you more responsible for high school. I have no doubt that YOU GOT THIS!

Journal

YOU
GOT
THIS!

Notes

blog.schoolspeciality.com (2020). The Benefits of Participation in After School Activities. Retrieved from https://blog.schoolspecialty.com/benefits-participation-school-activities/

cmhc.utexas.edu. (2020). Self-esteem. Retrieved from https://cmhc.utexas.edu/selfesteem.html#:~:text=Consequences%20of%20Low%20Self%2DEsteem,-Low%20self%2Desteem&text=create%20anxiety%2C%20stress%2C%20loneliness%2C,to%20drug%20and%20alcohol%20abuse

merriam-webster.com. (2020) pressure. Retrieved from https://www.merriam-webster.com/dictionary/peer%20pressure

verywellfamil.com (2020). Negative and Positive Peer Pressure Difference. Retrieved from https://www.verywellfamily.com/negative-and-positive-peer-pressure-differences-2606643

Made in the USA
Middletown, DE
26 January 2023